My Pl Words

Consultants

Ashley Bishop, Ed.D.

Sue Bishop, M.E.D.

Publishing Credits

Dona Herweck Rice, *Editor-in-Chief*

Robin Erickson, *Production Director*

Lee Aucoin, *Creative Director*

Sharon Coan, *Project Manager*

Jamey Acosta, *Editor*

Rachelle Cracchiolo, M.A.Ed., *Publisher*

Image Credits

cover Evgeny Karandaev/Shutterstock; p.2 shooarts/Shutterstock; p.3 Iurii Konoval/Shutterstock; p.4 ref348985/Shutterstock; p.5 Helder Almeida/Shutterstock; p.6 Valentyn Volkov/Shutterstock; p.7 Leftleg/Shutterstock; p.8 Carsten Reisinger/Shutterstock; p.9 Petr Malyshev/Shutterstock; p.10 Evgeny Karandaev/Shutterstock; back cover Valentyn Volkov/Shutterstock

---

Teacher Created Materials

5301 Oceanus Drive

Huntington Beach, CA 92649-1030

http://www.tcmpub.com

ISBN 978-1-4333-3981-3

Look at the plant.

Where is the plant?

Look at the plate.

Where is the plate?

Look at the plum.

Where are the plums?

Look at the plug.

Where is the plug?

Look at the pliers.

Glossary

plant

plate

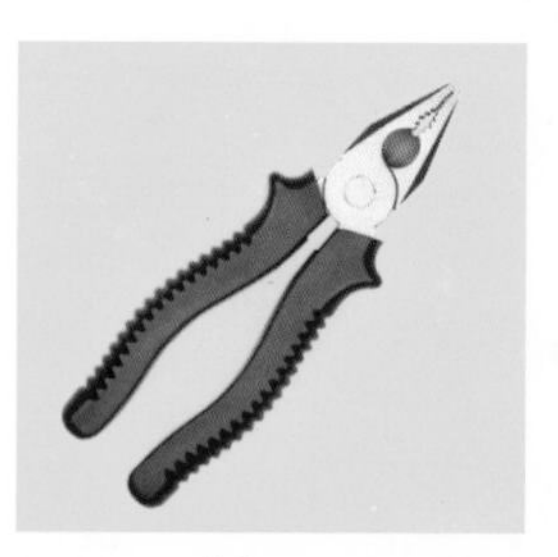

pliers

plug

plum

Sight Words

Look at the Where is are

Activities

- Read the book aloud to your child, pointing to the *pl* words. Help your child describe where the *pl* objects are found.
- Explain to your child the importance of not touching plugs or receptacles. Childproof your outlets and power strips with caps and covers.
- Compare your plates to shapes. Are they like circles, squares, or ovals?
- Have your child plant carrots, radishes, or lettuce and watch the plants grow.
- Have your child water the different plants as you discuss each plant's characteristics.
- Help your child think of a personally valuable word to represent the letters *pl*, such as *please*.